# THE MOVIE STORYBOOK

adapted by Rick Barba
based on the story by Michael Gordon and Stuart Beattie & Stephen Sommers
and the screenplay by Stuart Beattie and David Elliot & Paul Lovett

SIMON SPOTLIGHT
New York   London   Toronto   Sydney

Based on Hasbro's G.I. JOE® Characters

In a briefing room at the NATO headquarters in Brussels, Belgium, a group of army generals sat in the dark, listening to a man named Destro McCullen. McCullen was the owner of MARS Industries, a high-tech weapons company. He was telling them about the ultimate new superweapon. "Nanomites," McCullen said. "They're perfect little soldiers. They can do almost anything—eat a tank, for example."

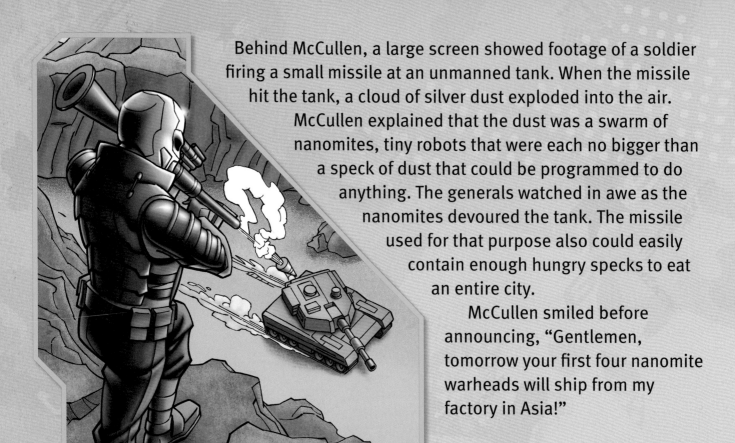

Behind McCullen, a large screen showed footage of a soldier firing a small missile at an unmanned tank. When the missile hit the tank, a cloud of silver dust exploded into the air. McCullen explained that the dust was a swarm of nanomites, tiny robots that were each no bigger than a speck of dust that could be programmed to do anything. The generals watched in awe as the nanomites devoured the tank. The missile used for that purpose also could easily contain enough hungry specks to eat an entire city.

McCullen smiled before announcing, "Gentlemen, tomorrow your first four nanomite warheads will ship from my factory in Asia!"

After the meeting one of the commanders, General Clayton "Hawk" Abernathy, offered to help protect the dangerous bomb shipment. The general was the head of a special unit of agents known as G.I. JOE.

But McCullen did not want any help. "Maybe next time, General," he said firmly, before making his exit.

When McCullen had left, General Hawk nodded to his aide, Cover Girl. She knew exactly what this meant: Get G.I. JOE ready to go!

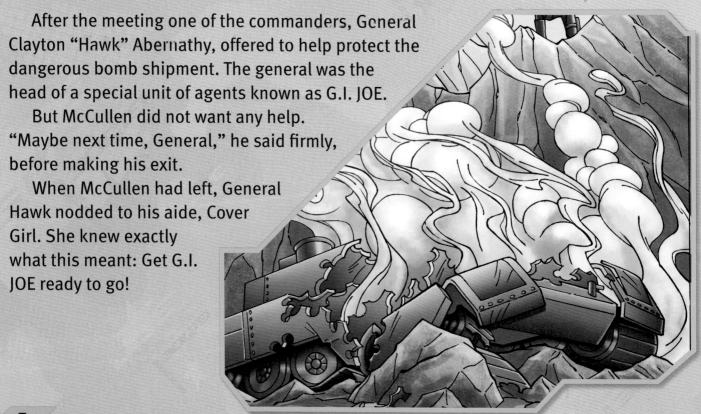

The next day a convoy of army trucks traveled down a hot, dusty road toward an air base in Central Asia. The trucks carried a team of NATO soldiers, led by Captain Conrad "Duke" Hauser and his partner, Lt. Wallace "Ripcord" Weems.

"I really want to fly jets someday, Duke," said Ripcord, looking up at the sky. "I want up in the air."

"You want up in the air?" Duke retorted. "I'll buy you a trampoline."

Duke and Ripcord rode in front of an armored Grizzly truck that carried the nanomite bombs—four softball-size glass spheres—in a small case. The bombs were not "weaponized" yet, meaning the nanomites inside were inactive, or "asleep."

Suddenly, a deadly black Typhoon gunship dropped in behind the convoy. *Boom!* Its powerful cannons hit truck after truck. Duke and Ripcord rolled out of their smashed Grizzly in time to see a squad of Viper soldiers, dressed head to toe in black battle armor, jump out of the aircraft.

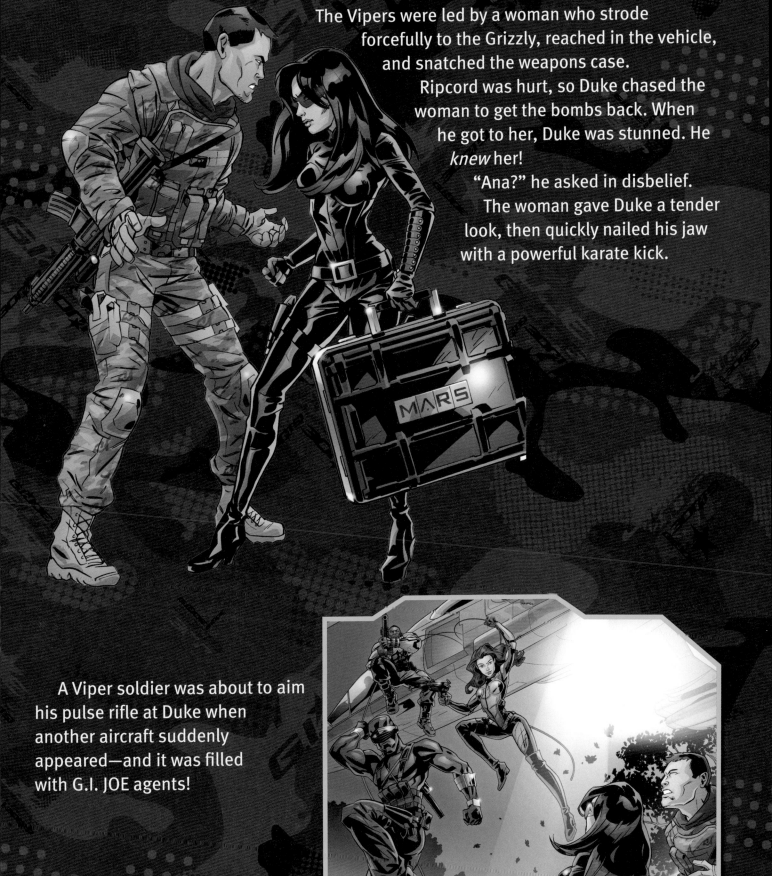

The Vipers were led by a woman who strode forcefully to the Grizzly, reached in the vehicle, and snatched the weapons case.

Ripcord was hurt, so Duke chased the woman to get the bombs back. When he got to her, Duke was stunned. He *knew* her!

"Ana?" he asked in disbelief.

The woman gave Duke a tender look, then quickly nailed his jaw with a powerful karate kick.

A Viper soldier was about to aim his pulse rifle at Duke when another aircraft suddenly appeared—and it was filled with G.I. JOE agents!

First out of the Howler transport ship was Snake Eyes, a ninja warrior. Then three others emerged: Scarlett, Heavy Duty, and Breaker. They wasted no time, defeating many Vipers and driving off the rest—including Ana, who left empty-handed.

Duke was relieved to retrieve the weapons case and find the nanomite bombs safe . . . for now.

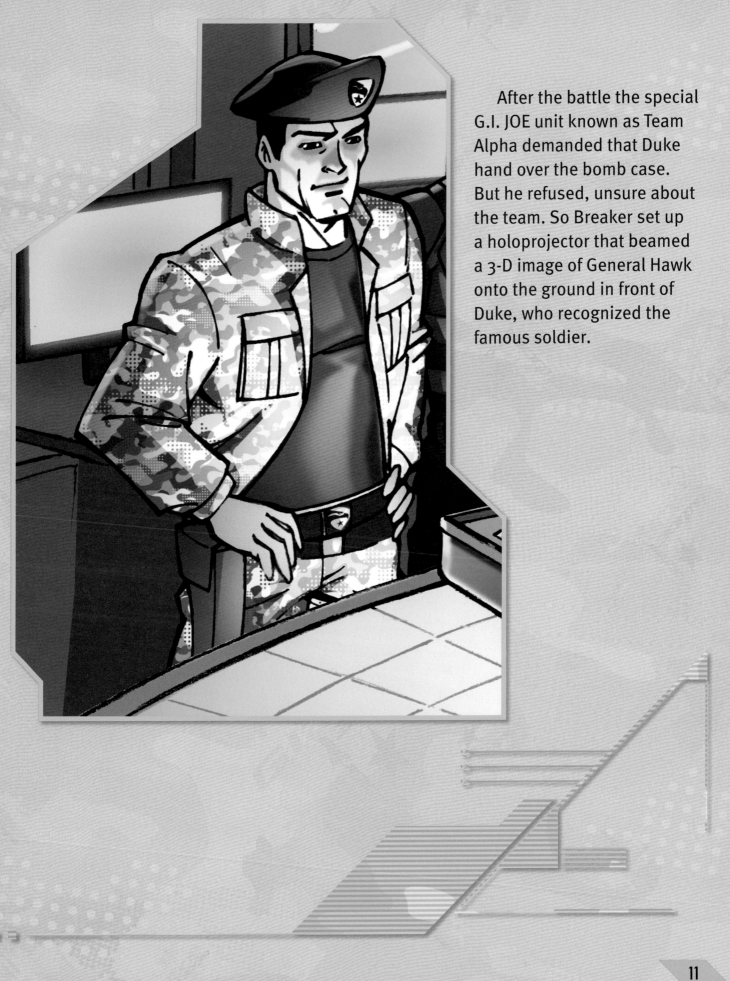

After the battle the special G.I. JOE unit known as Team Alpha demanded that Duke hand over the bomb case. But he refused, unsure about the team. So Breaker set up a holoprojector that beamed a 3-D image of General Hawk onto the ground in front of Duke, who recognized the famous soldier.

"My team just saved your life, son," the general said. "Hand over the case. We'll deliver the warheads."

"No way," Duke insisted. "It's *my* mission. I'll deliver them."

"Fine," General Hawk said. "Team Alpha will deliver you to me, then."

Duke and Ripcord agreed to travel with G.I. JOE, flying over the great pyramids of Giza to a secret underground base, known as the Pit, in the middle of the Egyptian desert.

In the Pit, General Hawk greeted Duke and Ripcord. "We have the best team of specialists from twenty-three nations training here," he declared proudly.

G.I. JOE agents were training in special areas of the base. Some were wearing camo-suits that allowed users to blend freely into any background. These nearly invisible team members moved through a citylike part of the Pit called the urban combat level.

Ripcord watched a woman zip into a camo-suit—and she disappeared right before his eyes. "Oh man, I want one of those," he said admiringly.

Other JOEs piloted fantastic underwater vehicles called SHARCs (submersible high-speed attack and reconnaissance craft) in the deep-sea combat level, a giant underground water tank.

Duke and Ripcord were impressed and excited. They wanted to be part of G.I. JOE!

In the Pit's control room General Hawk turned on another holoprojector, which beamed a 3-D image of Destro McCullen onto the floor.

"Meet the man who invented these nanomites," the general said.

McCullen's ghostly image stared at Duke as he spoke sternly. "Captain, I spent ten years and thirteen billion dollars creating these warheads," McCullen said. "Your job was to protect them. And you failed."

"My team did everything we could out there," Duke replied, trying not to show his anger. "Somebody sold us out."

But McCullen did not want to hear any more from Duke. He wanted the bombs delivered to NATO right away. However, General Hawk disagreed. He did not want them moved until his team could identify and track down the mysterious Vipers.

"All right," McCullen agreed, "but allow me to check the bombs."

McCullen gave him a special code—529440—that Breaker entered into a keypad on the bomb case. The case clicked open. When McCullen was satisfied that the warheads were not damaged, he cut off the holoprojector feed.

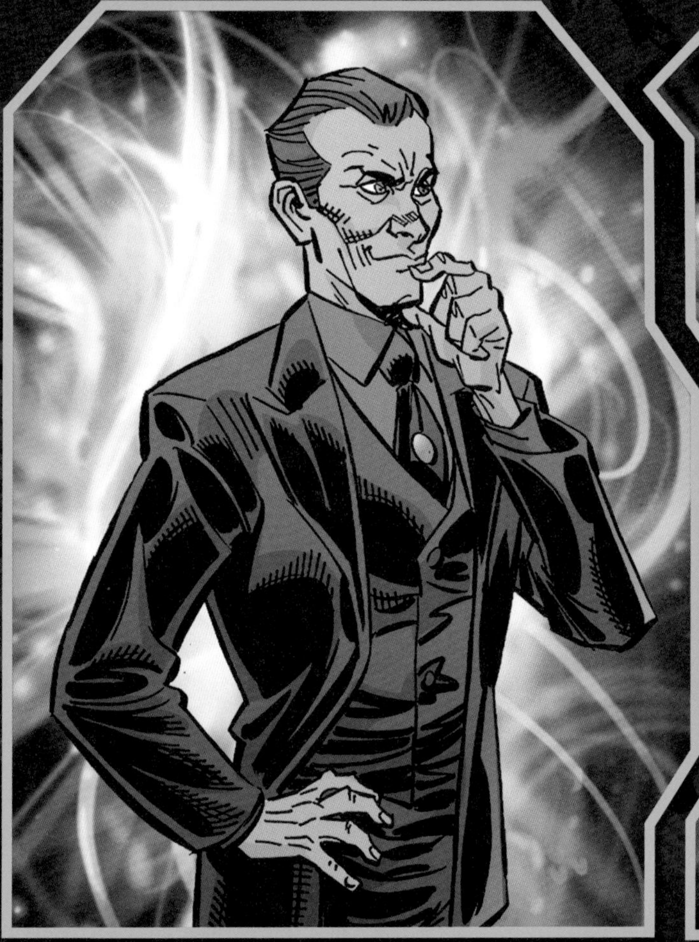 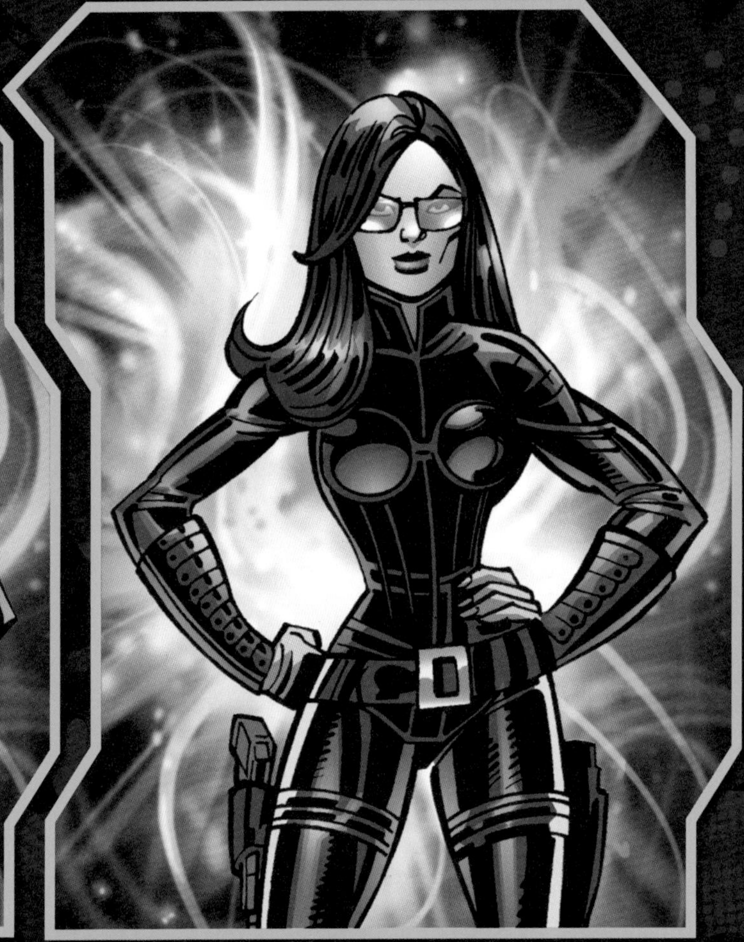

Little did General Hawk and the others know that McCullen was on a Trident submarine deep in the Arctic Ocean—standing next to Ana, the Viper leader who had tried to steal the nanomite bombs. It was McCullen himself who ordered the attack on Duke and the NATO soldiers!

"How can we find the bomb case now?" Ana asked.

"That unlocking code I just gave Hawk also turns on a beacon in the case," McCullen replied slyly. "It's a tracking signal."

He pointed to a computer screen, where a tiny green light had just started blinking on a map of the Egyptian desert. "Yes, there it is."

"The G.I. JOE base?" Ana asked.

"Exactly," McCullen answered, as the sub entered the docking bay of a huge underwater base. When Ana had left the ship, a ninja named Storm Shadow spoke up.

"If you'd sent me instead of her, we'd have the bombs back already," he told McCullen. Destro nodded. "I'm sending you now," he said. "And there can be no more mistakes."

A short while later McCullen met with a scientist known only as the Doctor, whose face was completely hidden behind a black life-support mask. He showed McCullen his newest creation: a team of soldiers called Neo Vipers. Injected with brain-changing nanomites, Neo Vipers obeyed every command without question.

"They feel no fear or pain," the Doctor reported. "They are completely obedient."

McCullen could not have been more pleased. "With an army of these soldiers *and* our warheads, we can unite the world," he said with a satisfied smirk.

Of course, what Destro McCullen meant by "unite the world" was this: He planned to use nanomites to scare the world into making him its supreme ruler.

Back at the Pit, Duke finally admitted to General Hawk and the other JOEs that he knew the woman who had led the ambush.

"Her name is Ana Lewis," Duke said, "and four years ago I nearly married her."

General Hawk and the others were stunned.

"Can you defeat her if necessary?" the general asked, watching Duke carefully.

Duke rubbed his jaw, still feeling Ana's karate kick. "Yes," he said grimly.

Ripcord glanced at Duke. Four years ago Duke and Ana had parted ways, and they had not seen each other since. But Ripcord suspected that, deep down, his friend still loved Ana.

The next day Duke and Ripcord began their G.I. JOE training. First, Heavy Duty fitted them with Mark One Accelerator Suits. These suits helped the JOEs run superfast, jump superhigh, and punch superhard.

"I've never seen combat gear like this," Duke said, flexing his arms with ease. "What's the secret?"

"Liquid armor," Heavy Duty replied.

Ripcord jumped ten feet into the air. "Wow!" he exclaimed. "How do I look? Pretty cool, huh?"

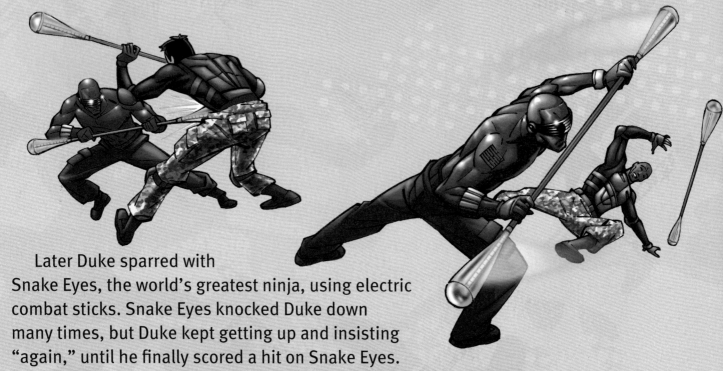

Later Duke sparred with
Snake Eyes, the world's greatest ninja, using electric
combat sticks. Snake Eyes knocked Duke down
many times, but Duke kept getting up and insisting
"again," until he finally scored a hit on Snake Eyes.

Breaker was shocked. "I have *never, ever* seen Snake Eyes take a hit!"

At the same time Ripcord impressed Scarlett with his fast work against targets on the
G.I. JOE obstacle course. The other team members had to admit that these two newcomers
were pretty good agents.

After the testing General Hawk announced that both
Duke and Ripcord had passed. In fact, Duke had some of
the highest scores ever!

"Welcome aboard!" General Hawk said.

That night several Mole Pod drilling vehicles chewed right through the rock walls of the Pit. Once inside, the pods opened up. Ana, Storm Shadow, and a group of Neo Vipers fell out!

Using a special scanning device, Ana called out, "This way!" and then led her team to General Hawk's office. Storm Shadow struck the surprised commander before Ana ripped General Hawk's security badge off his jacket and used it to unlock his special vault.

Inside the vault Ana found the case with the nanomite bombs.

"Excellent!" she exclaimed.

But as Ana grabbed the case, General Hawk suddenly rolled over and pressed an alarm button. Loud emergency sirens started to blare!

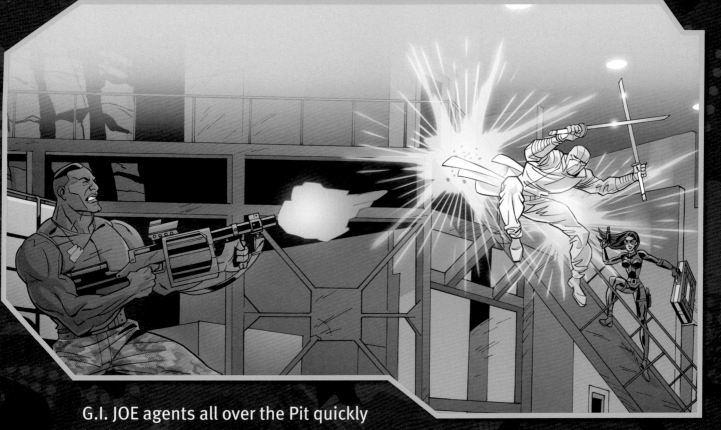

G.I. JOE agents all over the Pit quickly rushed into action. Heavy Duty used his grenade launcher to blow up the enemy Mole Pods. Now the intruders couldn't use them to escape. Then Duke and Ripcord arrived, as did Snake Eyes, who came face-to-face with his old ninja enemy, Storm Shadow.

"Hello, *brother*," Storm Shadow said.

It was ninja-versus-ninja action as the two fought with swords that swung and jabbed at impossibly fast speeds!

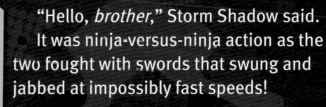

While the ninja battle raged, Duke had Ana trapped on a gangway. "Put down the bomb case, Ana," he ordered.

"You won't stop me," she said, "because deep down, you're still the same man I fell in love with."

"Don't listen to her, Duke!" Ripcord shouted.

Suddenly, Duke was hit with the blast of a Neo Viper pulse pistol—and Ana took off with the bomb case!

Storm Shadow finally eluded Snake Eyes's attacks and slipped into the harness of an arclight jetpack. He flew over Ana, grabbed her, and zoomed up the Pit's elevator shaft.

At the top Ana blasted open the ceiling with her pulse gun, and, with their jetpack, Storm Shadow and Ana glided out into the cold desert night. Then they hopped aboard their waiting Typhoon gunship and escaped across the Egyptian desert.

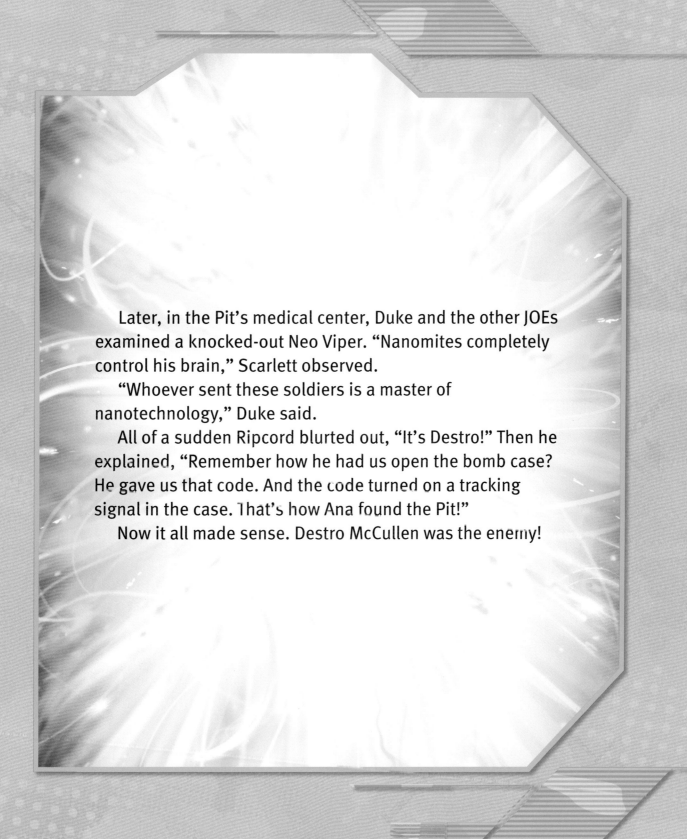

Later, in the Pit's medical center, Duke and the other JOEs examined a knocked-out Neo Viper. "Nanomites completely control his brain," Scarlett observed.

"Whoever sent these soldiers is a master of nanotechnology," Duke said.

All of a sudden Ripcord blurted out, "It's Destro!" Then he explained, "Remember how he had us open the bomb case? He gave us that code. And the code turned on a tracking signal in the case. That's how Ana found the Pit!"

Now it all made sense. Destro McCullen was the enemy!

Just then Breaker rushed in with more news. "I did an online photo match of Ana's image," he said. "Follow me!"

In the control room Breaker displayed a profile of the Baroness, Ana DeCobray. Her husband, Leon, was a French baron and well-known scientist whose Paris lab operated a special machine called a particle accelerator.

"Particle accelerator?" Scarlett wondered out loud. "Destro can use that to weaponize his warheads!"

"Right, and that's where Ana is taking the bomb case right now," Duke said. "Let's go!"

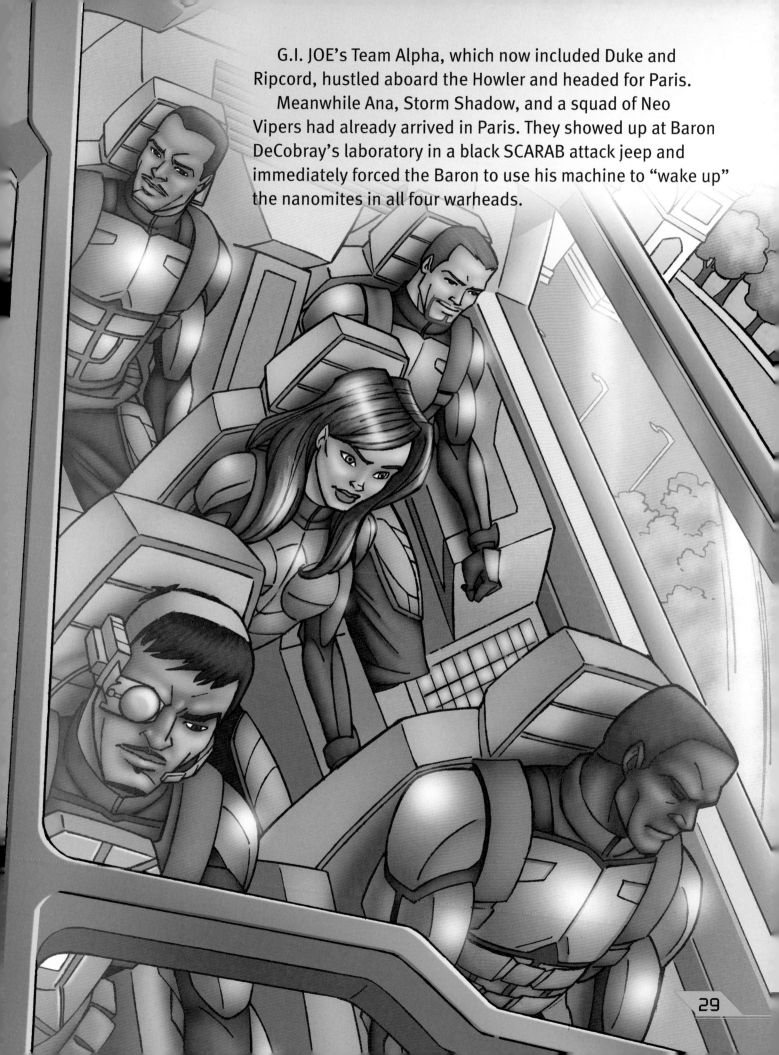

G.I. JOE's Team Alpha, which now included Duke and Ripcord, hustled aboard the Howler and headed for Paris. Meanwhile Ana, Storm Shadow, and a squad of Neo Vipers had already arrived in Paris. They showed up at Baron DeCobray's laboratory in a black SCARAB attack jeep and immediately forced the Baron to use his machine to "wake up" the nanomites in all four warheads.

G.I. JOE was a tad late, getting to DeCobray's lab in their Brawler armored truck just as the enemy SCARAB was leaving. But this didn't stop the JOEs.

"Yo, JOEs!" Heavy Duty hollered as he drove the Brawler. "Let's go!"

It was time for G.I. JOE action! Duke and Ripcord put on their accelerator suits, leaped out of the Brawler, and chased the black SCARAB on foot, jumping over cars and racing at high speed through oncoming traffic. They fired their wrist-mounted rockets at the fleeing SCARAB. Protected by their armored suits, they even smashed through the walls of a building.

Inside the Brawler, Breaker and Scarlett studied an onscreen map, trying to figure out where the black SCARAB was headed. Then Scarlett looked up—and realized what the SCARAB's target was.

"Guys, you have to stop them!" she shouted into her radio com-link.

"Yeah, we're working on it," Duke replied as he hurdled over a city bus.

"I mean *right now*," said Scarlett. "They're going to bomb the Eiffel Tower!"

Up ahead, the speeding SCARAB crossed a train track and crashed into a commuter train! Although injured, Ana and Storm Shadow managed to escape the heavily armored truck and rushed toward the famous tower. The ninja wasted no time loading one of the nanomite bombs into a rocket launcher.

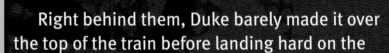

Right behind them, Duke barely made it over the top of the train before landing hard on the city street. Not realizing he could jump over the train, Ripcord dove through a window on one side of the train . . . and smashed through a window on the other side, tumbling on the street next to Duke and the mangled SCARAB.

Ana and Storm Shadow charged into an office building across from the Eiffel Tower carrying the nanomite weapon and the kill switch. Minutes later Duke and Ripcord made their way to the building as well.

Ripcord took off after Storm Shadow, who was running up a spiral staircase with the weapon. The ninja quickly found an office that directly faced the world-famous tower and took aim. Ripcord tried to stop Storm Shadow, but he was too late! The weapon struck its target, and the nanomites immediately went to work—attacking the base of the tower. His work done, Storm Shadow escaped.

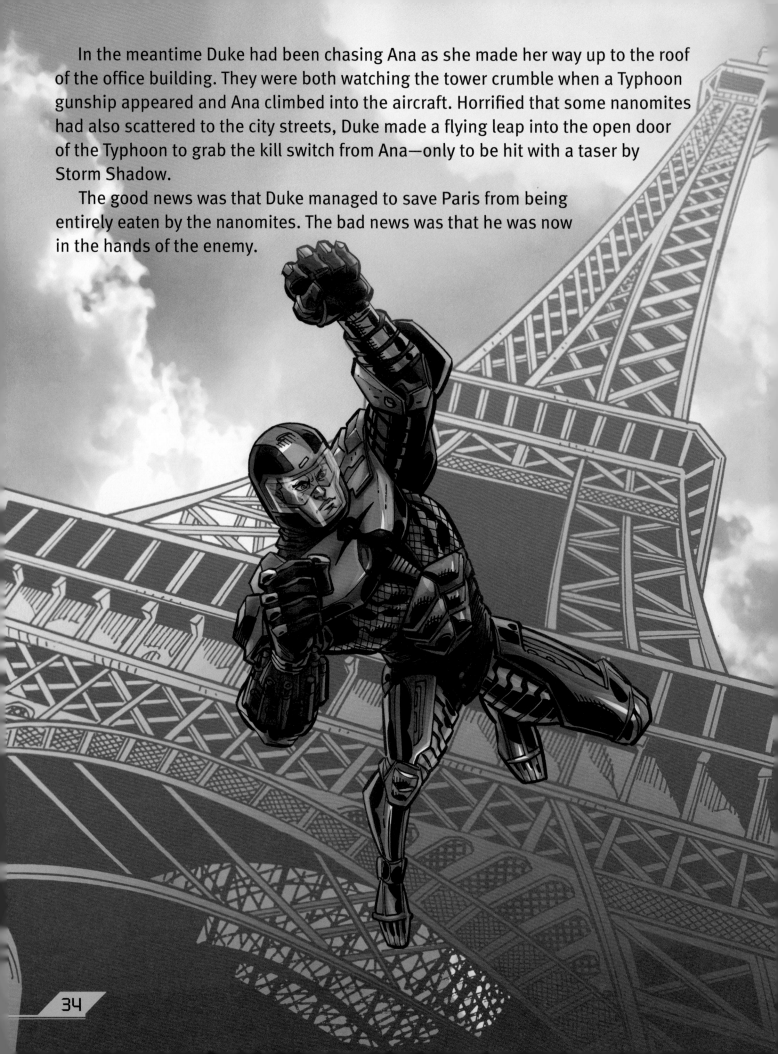

In the meantime Duke had been chasing Ana as she made her way up to the roof of the office building. They were both watching the tower crumble when a Typhoon gunship appeared and Ana climbed into the aircraft. Horrified that some nanomites had also scattered to the city streets, Duke made a flying leap into the open door of the Typhoon to grab the kill switch from Ana—only to be hit with a taser by Storm Shadow.

The good news was that Duke managed to save Paris from being entirely eaten by the nanomites. The bad news was that he was now in the hands of the enemy.

On the ground, the French police immediately arrested the G.I. JOE team members, thinking they were the criminals who had destroyed their beloved Eiffel Tower.

While in jail, Ripcord worried about Duke as Breaker, Heavy Duty, and Scarlett studied an image of Ana boarding the Typhoon gunship at her snowy base.

"Lots of snow," Heavy Duty observed. "So that narrows it down to about . . . a third of the globe."

"But look," Breaker said, "we can see the sun *and* her shadow."

Scarlett smiled. "Spherical trigonometry," she said, as Ripcord looked puzzled. "To find a latitude and longitude, all you need to know is the height of an object, the length of its shadow, and the time and date when the image was recorded," Scarlett explained.

"It's the polar ice cap," Breaker said, after doing some quick calculations. "Destro's base is at the North Pole."

Just then General Hawk appeared, confined to a wheelchair after the attack at the Pit. The team was glad to see him, although the news he had for them was grim.

"The French government is allowing you to leave on the condition that you never return. We are to shut down . . . and report to Washington."

"That's it? They've got Duke!" Ripcord shouted in disbelief.

"I said you were to report to Washington. I didn't say when or which route to take," the general added slyly before wheeling out the door.

In the meantime Ana and Storm Shadow arrived at McCullen's underwater Arctic base with their prisoner and the remaining three nanomite warheads. It looked hopeless for Duke. There was nothing but ice for hundreds of miles in every direction.

But Duke was not giving up just yet. He grabbed the bomb case from Ana and started to run—only to have Storm Shadow quickly knock him down. But before the Neo Vipers reached Duke, he secretly tapped Destro's beacon code into the case's number keypad—529440—and no one saw him do it!

"What was your plan?" Storm Shadow asked with a sneer. "Run three thousand miles across the ice?"

McCullen ordered the warheads to be mounted onto aerial drones and prepared for launch. Then he took Duke to meet the Doctor.

"Here's another recruit for our army," McCullen told the scientist.

"I'll prepare him for the procedure," the Doctor said, eager to inject Duke with nasty nanomites and turn him into another mindless Neo Viper.

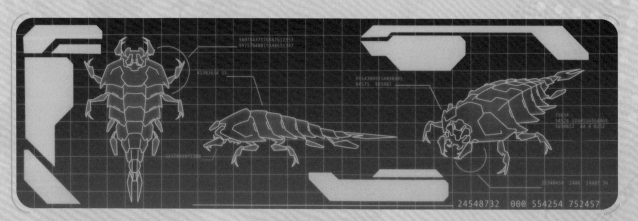

Before long a sleek G.I. JOE submarine was making its way toward the North Pole, carrying a large company of agents, including Team Alpha. The area of the polar ice cap was so massive that Breaker was not sure where to start looking for McCullen's base—until he saw something flashing on his radar map.

"Hey, that's the tracker beacon from the bomb case!" he said, puzzled.

Ripcord realized that Duke must have turned it on. "That's my boy," he said with a wide grin. There was hope yet!

The beacon led them right to the enemy base, which was protected by a gigantic turbo-pulse cannon that could shatter any ship with a single blast. Once onshore Scarlett, Snake Eyes, Breaker, and Ripcord climbed onto their Rock Slide combat snowmobiles and traced the tracker beacon to an ice cave.

The cave had a secret elevator shaft and a black Night Raven, a big, supersonic ram-jet aircraft capable of flying at three times the speed of sound. Ripcord looked in awe at the aircraft as Scarlett ordered, "Let's get down that shaft!"

But it was too late!

McCullen had launched all three aerial drones. The first two rockets rose through the ice and thundered off in different directions—one toward Moscow, and the other toward Washington, D.C. But as the third drone rose, Snake Eyes shot it down with heat-seeking rockets fired from his Rock Slide. Only two bombs left!

"Somebody has to shoot those things down!" Scarlett yelled as she watched the vapor trails of the first two drones.

"That's me," Ripcord volunteered immediately.

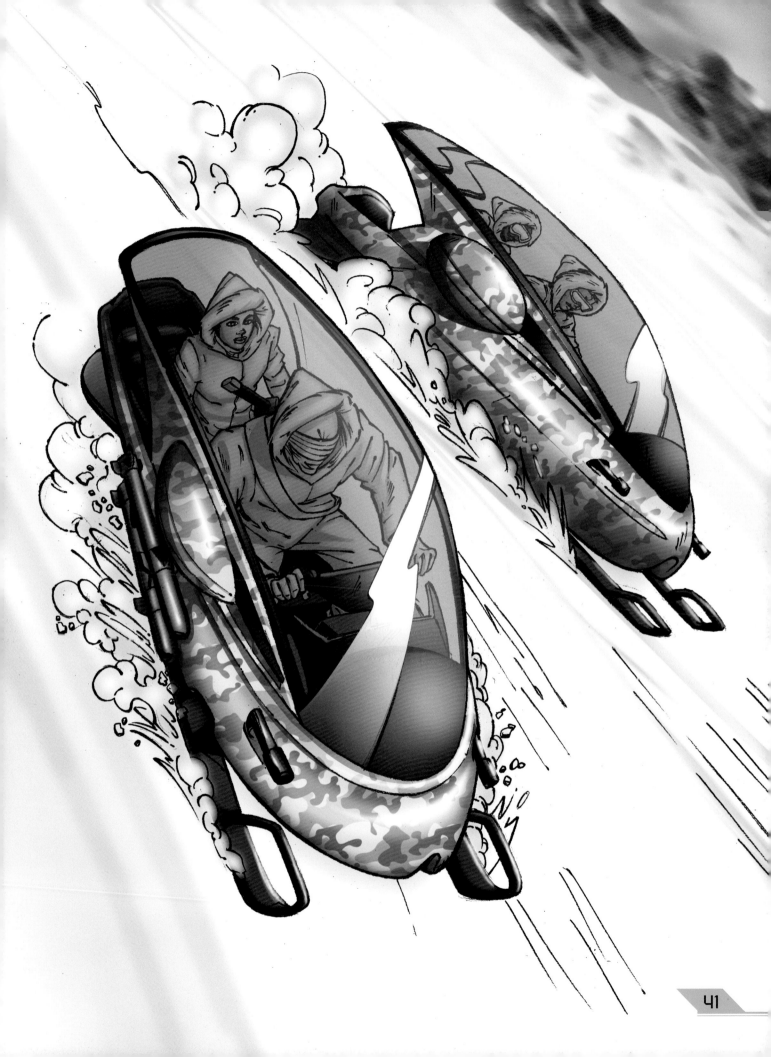

Jumping into the Night Raven's cockpit,
Ripcord flipped a few switches and took off.
First he targeted and destroyed the drone
streaking toward Moscow. The nanomites
scattered harmlessly into the upper atmosphere.
Then he swung the Night Raven west and rocketed
at full speed toward the final drone.

Could he reach it in time?

Back at McCullen's Arctic base, the Doctor was about to turn Duke into a zombielike Neo Viper when Ana suddenly appeared—and released him! Angered, the Doctor knocked her out with a control device just before McCullen showed up.

Using one of Ana's pistols, Duke fired a blast that burned McCullen's face. The Doctor immediately dragged the badly injured McCullen to an escape vehicle, while Duke took Ana to safety.

In a Trident submarine, the Doctor injected McCullen with nanomites, which began to create a mask that fit perfectly over his badly burned face.

McCullen fell to his knees, screaming. He was shocked at what was happening, but quickly realized that the nanomites were saving him. "I guess I should thank you, Doctor," he said weakly.

The Doctor did not respond right away. He was busy entering information into a personal device. Then, putting his own mask on, he told McCullen, "From now on, I'll be on a first-name basis with you, Destro. And I want you to call me . . . Commander."

"Yes, Commander," McCullen replied mechanically.

Not far away, Snake Eyes managed to slip past laser security nets and disable the turbo-pulse cannon. Snake Eyes sent a text message to Heavy Duty back on the sub:

CANNON OFF-LINE, HAVE A NICE DAY

When Heavy Duty read it, he grinned and said, "Let's get in this fight!"

He led a team of agents down to the sub's launch bay in dozens of SHARCs, defeating the Neo Viper force. Soon the bad guys were on the run!

Far away, high in the air, the Night Raven was streaking through the North American sky, closing in on the final speeding nanomite drone. The warhead was now just seconds from wiping out Washington, D.C.

"You're too close, Rip," Breaker called on his radio. "Back up!"

"Actually," said Ripcord, "I think I'm just close enough."

Ripcord took careful aim—closer, closer—then fired the Raven's laser pulse guns.

It was a direct hit! The final drone was blown to pieces.

But the nanomites started swarming the Night Raven and eating the plane! Ripcord pulled back on the control stick and flew the deadly dust high into the upper atmosphere, where the nanomites were harmless—before ejecting himself from the plane.

Moments later he landed his parachute safely on the White House lawn. Ripcord was a hero!

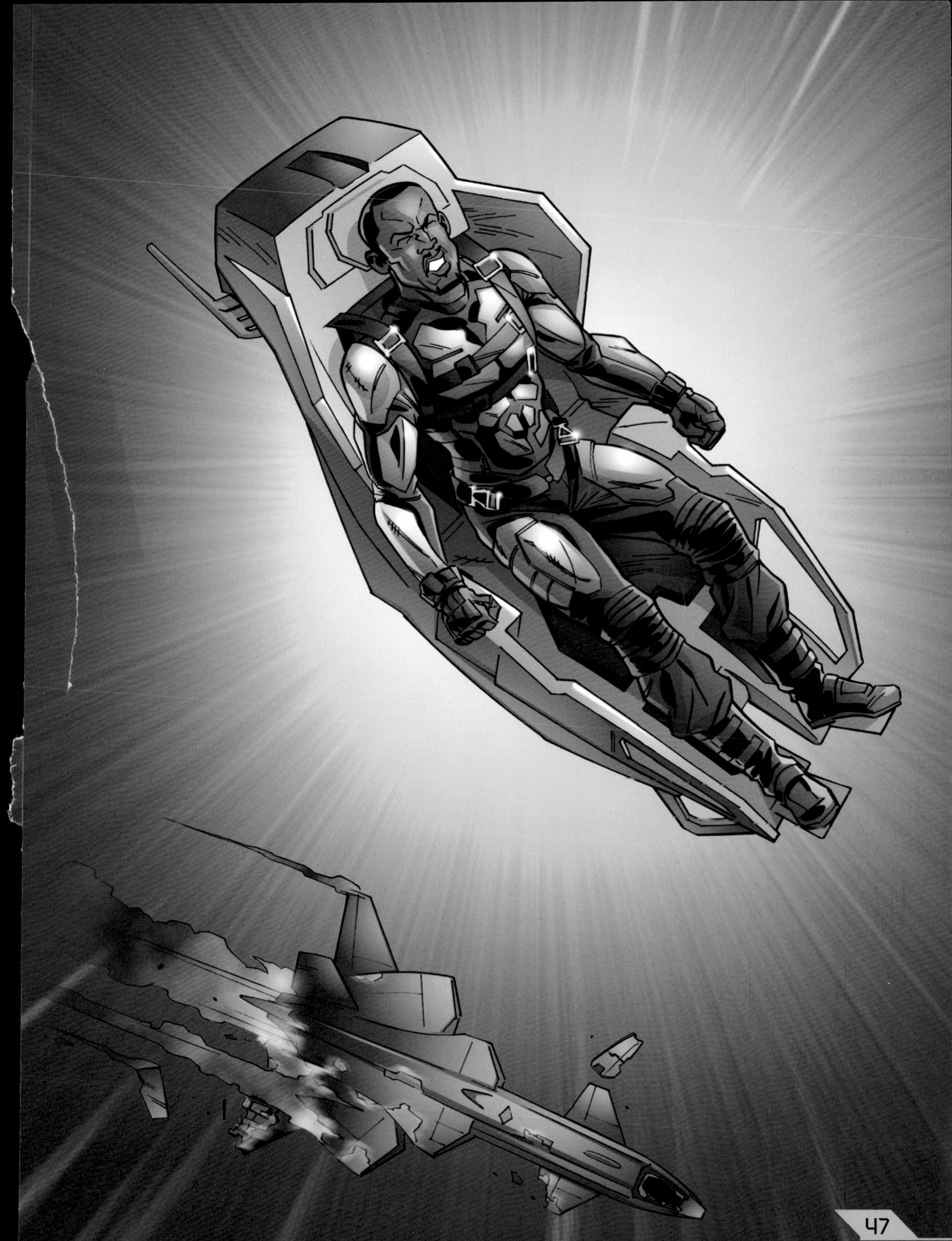

Back at the Pit, General Hawk congratulated G.I. JOE for a job well done. "Heavy Duty says you boys should stick around," he told Duke and Ripcord.

"That's what we're planning, sir," said Duke. "Right, Rip?"

"I'm good," Ripcord replied with a wink.

Everyone laughed and climbed aboard their Howler jet. As Heavy Duty and Breaker slammed the hatch shut, they gave the G.I. JOE cry: "Yo, JOE!"